Our Little Boer Cousin

Luna May Innes

Copyright © 2023 Culturea Editions
Text and cover : © public domain
Edition : Culturea (Hérault, 34)
Contact : infos@culturea.fr
Print in Germany by Books on Demand
Design and layout : Derek Murphy
Layout : Reedsy (https://reedsy.com/)
ISBN : 9791041826049
Légal deposit : July 2023

Our Little Boer Cousin

CHAPTER I

PETRUS JOUBERT

It was spring in the Transvaal. Already the wattle-trees beside the farm-schoolhouse door were thickly covered with a mass of golden bloom, and the little blue pan — or lake — down among the willows, again reflected the sky and clouds as the Boer children trooped past it.

Many a chilly morning had they trudged on their way to that same little room of corrugated iron and wood, just beyond the farthest kopje — often so early that the grass was still sparkling with the sunlit hoar-frost.

The sun shone warm now, and groups of laughing little Boer girls, in large pinafores and kappies, hurried across the trackless grassy veldt from every direction. Some of them, like Christina Allida, Adriana, Franzina, and black-eyed, laughing little Yettie, whose farms were a long way off, drove over in their crowded Cape cart spiders and ramshackle conveyances of every description.

Soon Franzina's cart, with Yettie, came rumbling up to the door, where all the older boys — like their big cousin, Petrus Joubert — who had galloped over on their shaggy little Cape ponies, were off-saddling and knee-haltering them under the wattle-trees. To remove the saddle, and then, with the head-stall, to fasten the pony's head to his leg just above his knee, so that he might graze freely about, yet be caught again when wanted after school was out, took but a moment. Then the saddles were hung on the schoolhouse wall in a lengthening row, and lessons begun.

All Boer boys are trained to ride from the time they can walk. Petrus could even "out-spann" a team of his uncle's oxen. He was fond of all animals — especially of his sturdy little Basuto pony, which he had christened "Ferus." Ferus meant "fearless." He prized him above everything he possessed. He was trained to obey the slightest turn of the reins, or to come to a full stop at the sound of one low whistle from his master. Through storm or sunshine he carried his young rider swiftly to school and home again — always with little five-year-old brother Theunis holding tightly on behind.

"Jump, Theunis!" affectionately called Petrus to the child. Theunis, his only brother, was very dear to him.

Still clutching a dog-eared copy of "Steb-by-Steb" in one small hand, Theunis slid off and hurried after his big brother into the little room.

Soon it was crowded with noisy children, all busily buzzing over their English lessons, and answering "Ek-weit-nie" to the teacher's questions. It was a government farm-school. Only one hour a day was allowed for Dutch.

Petrus would be ready for the High School at Johannesburg in the fall. He was one of the brightest boys in the school. Not only did he head his classes, but he had read the Bible and "Steps of Youth" — two books all Boer boys study — well — twice through. Also, he was perfectly familiar with the "Stories from Homer" and the "History of the United States of America." This last book, like his Bible, he never could read enough. Its story of the struggle for liberty, by a brave people like his own, against the same hostile power his ancestors for generations had had to combat, fascinated him.

In the Transvaal's mild, sub-tropical climate, with its wonderful health-giving air, the Boer youth develops early into self-reliant manhood. At thirteen Petrus was nearly as tall as his Uncle Abraham, and was more than the physical equal of his English or American cousins of sixteen or seventeen. Living a healthy outdoor farm-life, he had become a great broad-shouldered lad of strong stalwart build, with the resolute forward tread of his "voor-trekking" ancestors.

One could see that Petrus was a true "Hollander-Boer" — from his corduroy trousers and the large home-made "veldt-schoens" on his feet, to the broad-brimmed hat that shaded his fair hair and blue eyes from the African sun. Yet there was a certain French-Huguenot cast to his features. It came from the Jouberts on his father's side of the family. Some of the brightest pages of the Transvaal's history had been written by a brave soldier uncle of his — Petrus Joubert — whose great-great-grandfather had fled from France to South Africa with hundreds of his persecuted countrymen for freedom to read his Bible and to worship among the Dutch Boers of the Transvaal. He became one of them, fought in their wars, was made their president, and later they appointed him commandant-general of all the Boer forces when hostilities began against England. Petrus was his namesake. Of this he was very proud. His family called him "Koos" for short.

From his school desk near the window, Petrus kept a wolf-like eye on his pony as he grazed about. Sometimes Ferus wandered entirely out of sight. This always distressed Petrus greatly.

As he gazed across the high veldt for miles about, Petrus could almost see the outskirts of his uncle's vast farm of six thousand acres. First, beyond a few scattered red-brown kopjes, there was the blue pan—then, just beyond—through a small plantation of Scotch firs and poplars—he could see the plain little Dutch Reformed Church, which his uncle had re-roofed after the war. Still farther beyond was Johannesburg, the "Golden City," where he had been promised he might attend High School next winter. The thought thrilled him. How good his uncle had always been to him, he thought. There on the farm, with his uncle and Aunt Johanna, his grandfather and great-grandfather, he had lived ever since he could remember. His own dear father had been killed in the war. His mother had scarcely survived the hardships of the terrible time when their house and everything they owned had been burned to the ground by British soldiers. Then his kind Uncle Abraham—his mother's brother, who was an Elder in the Church—had welcomed them to his great place, "Weltefreden," the only home Petrus had ever known.

There was a loud ringing of the school bell. It was the noon hour. Out the children rushed helter-skelter—the girls to their games of "Frott" or "touch-wood," Petrus and the boys to their cricket and Rugby football.

"Oh, there's Uncle Abraham coming now!" exclaimed Petrus, with a start, as he saw a familiar pair of shaggy brown horses and a green cart rattling up to the schoolhouse door. Petrus ran to meet him.

"I come to say I must take Petrus to the farm to-day. The locusts are on my corn-fields, and my head Kafir is gone," explained Mr. Joubert to the teacher.

"But, Mr. Joubert, his inspection is coming off so soon," protested the teacher.

"I think one day will make no difference," persisted the uncle. "Petrus must come."

Further protest was useless. Petrus was allowed to climb quickly into his uncle's cart. Theunis would ride Ferus home.

The horses dashed through the deep grass of the high veldt, taking the shortest route home. Petrus could already see a blackening cloud in the distance overcasting the sky.

"Nothing will be left of my crops! — nothing!" excitedly exclaimed his uncle. "There is no time to be lost! Terrible swarms cover everything! My Kafirs are doing what they can, and your Aunt Johanna and some of the neighbors are holding a prayer-service for relief from the pests. We must be quick and add our prayers to theirs, else all will be lost!"

"Yes, yes, Uncle!" agreed Petrus quickly, thinking of his well-worn Testament. "It is terrible! But God will surely send us relief from this pestilence."

There was a muddy drift to be crossed. The wheels sank deep. Emerging safely on the opposite side, the team plunged directly ahead. Suddenly their way was obscured before them. The enormous flight had completely darkened the mid-day sun. Above their heads floated myriads of the insects in a great blackening mass. As Uncle Abraham tried to force the team through it, they filled the cart, beating against its sides and against their faces with a loud humming sound. Locusts are the great scourge of South Africa.

In the sudden gloom a herd of Lieutenant Wortley's fine cattle, crossing their path, was scarcely visible. Nor did they hear the lieutenant himself, and his little son George, calling to them.

"Oh, Uncle Abraham, here comes Lieutenant Wortley and George. They are waving to us to stop for them. Can't we, Uncle?"

Uncle Abraham hastily stopped the cart and welcomed his English friends. They were his nearest neighbors. Whatever hostile feelings he might once have had towards the British had long been forgotten. Thirteen years had passed since the war.

"Good day, Lieutenant Wortley. Here is plenty of room in the cart. Petrus, make room for George there with you. We are making all speed, Lieutenant, to save my crops from the locusts. We are going to have a big 'grass-burning' to-night, and smoke out whatever remain of the pests."

"Oh, Lieutenant Wortley, please let George stay with us for the burning! We always have such fine good times at a big grass-burning!" vehemently pleaded Petrus. "And I'll promise to ride home with him on Ferus, afterwards, and we'll—oh, what is that?"

Z-z-zip! Wh-i-zz! A great shower of gleaming Zulu assegais flew through the air over the cart.

Z-z-zip! came another past George's head. They hit the car with a metallic sound, glanced off and fell to earth.

"The Zulus! the Zulus!" cried the Englishman, seizing George close in his arms. "They have threatened our lives! The cowards! They are taking advantage of the dark. Quick, George, get down out of sight in the bottom of the cart! I'll fire at the villains!"

Bang! Boom! Bang! sounded the lieutenant's rifle.

The Zulus yelled, and quickly sent another shower of assegais. Petrus lowered his head. One landed heavily in the flying cart close to his feet. It was six feet long—its sharp iron head or blade being over a foot long in itself. An ox-tail ornamented the opposite end of the great spear. Already the darkening flight of locusts had passed on, leaving the sky bright and clear. Petrus gave one quick backward glance. One Zulu had fallen. The others were in hot pursuit.

Uncle Abraham lashed the horses into a wild gallop. The lieutenant again took careful aim and fired. The Zulus went tumbling back into the tall grass.

"They're afraid of our fire-arms! Hurrah!" cried Petrus in joy. "Hurrah! George, you're safe! They are gone!"

"Yes, thank heavens! We've escaped their poisoned assegais so far—the savages! I know that giant Zulu who was in the lead. I know him well. He is Dirk," continued the lieutenant. "He looked me straight in the eye, as he passed close and drew his assegai. No, Petrus, I'll take George home to-night. He's safer there. George thanks you just the same, but he has had a terrible fright. I don't mean to let my boy out of my sight."

The lieutenant lifted George—white and trembling—into his arms.

"Why, Lieutenant Wortley, should the Zulus threaten your lives?" demanded Mr. Joubert, as mystified as was Petrus.

"Yes, tell us," added Petrus—in suspense to hear.

"As you may know," began the Englishman, glad to make explanations, "my appointment as collector of His Majesty's 'Hunt-tax' followed the peace negotiations upon the close of the war. My first commission was to the Kalahari Desert—that great 'Thirst-land'—as it is called, covering thousands of miles of the most desolate, sandy, waterless, tract of land under the heavens. There—in that fearful spot—men, horses, and oxen are constantly dying of thirst—their skeletons by thousands strew the great hot sand stretches. George's mother had returned with him to our old home in England. After her death there, George's Aunt Edith brought the boy as far as Cape Town to me. I protested, but George—hungering for adventure—begged to be taken along with me. Finally, I consented.

"It was my official duty to collect the 'Hunt-tax.' I found that many of the savages of this God-forsaken region had never before paid a 'tax' of any kind. They rebelled. Among such was this giant Zulu—Dirk. He promptly refused to pay, although his horses were overloaded with the finest skins, ivory, and the longest koodoo horns I have ever seen.

"It was the climax of impudence when he disputed my authority and tried to argue with me. I had him promptly disarmed and jailed by two of my native police, afterwards ordering him put at convict work. He was set at well-digging, under guard, in the desert. It was a rough job, but my police accomplished it. Then it was that Dirk flung out that threat against our lives. There was something in his look and voice that made my blood run cold. To this day the mere sight of him makes me apprehensive. The threat was aimed at George as much as at me. George is always begging me to take him home to England. I may decide to do it."

"Oh, George dear! Don't you leave us! Never shall that Zulu harm you! I am a good marksman. I would shoot him before he should harm you! Never fear, George, I will be your protector always," vehemently cried the Boer boy.

Uncle Abraham shook his head gravely. They had reached the great farm. Bidding their friends adieu, Uncle Abraham and Petrus turned their attention to the locusts. They had settled themselves over the whole two miles of Uncle Abraham's tender, young mealie-fields in layers ten to twelve inches deep, and were busily mowing down the juicy stalks acre by acre.

CHAPTER II

AT "WELTEFREDEN"

Spring had passed. It was sweltering hot by noonday in the Transvaal, for the midsummer days of December had come. Christmas, with its tennis, golf, and gay "cross-country" riding parties, was but a few short weeks off. Petrus had missed George's visits to "Weltefreden" greatly. It was a long time since he had been there.

At first the terrible scare from the Zulus had thrown him into a violent fever, from which he had not recovered for weeks. After that the lieutenant had kept him closely at home. Of course Petrus had visited him there. He had also often sent him over good things from the farm, by Mutla, his favorite Kafir. Now that George was better Petrus half hoped each day to see him at the farm.

The Joubert household arose early mornings. Aunt Johanna always had breakfast by six. Then there was an hour's rest in the hottest part of the day, right after dinner. Petrus was the first one to be up and out enjoying the balmy morning air — watching the Kafir herders feeding the flocks, milking the cows, yoking the oxen, and driving the horses and sheep off to pasture. The vast farm, with its miles of waving grain and mealie-fields, and rolling pasture lands, was one of the best cultivated in all the Transvaal. It was a model farm.

The original little "wattle-and-daub" cottage, with its windows half hidden under creepers, was gone. In it Petrus had been born. Many years ago it had been replaced by a more pretentious homestead. Uncle Abraham had prospered. His huge granaries were always well-filled, and his Kafir farm boys, at the kraals, just beyond the mealie-fields, numbered more than a hundred. It was their work to milk the cows, care for the beasts, and attend to the hardest work of the farm.

Every morning, after breakfast, Uncle Abraham assembled the whole family for prayers, which Grandfather Joubert read with a simple impressiveness. Then a hymn was sung, and the family separated to take up their various tasks for the day.

It was Petrus' especial duty to mend all the broken-down wagons, make the halters and head-stalls for the ponies and horses, and, when hippopotamus hide could be procured, to cut and make the long lashes for the ox-whips. These were usually twenty-five feet long. Sometimes Mutla, his favorite Kafir, could find time to help him.

So, the first thing after breakfast, Petrus busied himself steeping bullock's hide in water. Uncle Abraham had told him that the Kafirs were needing more whip-cord and leather rope. Then Petrus took it from the water, cut it into narrow strips about ten feet long, greased and bound it together into one long piece, after which he took it out and hung it from a high tree-branch, first weighting the lower end with a heavy wagon-wheel. When it was thoroughly stretched he took it down, twisted all the grease and moisture out of it, scraped it until it became supple, and then put it away for every kind of use on the farm.

It was still early, so Petrus got out some large pieces of untanned leather. In the art of making "veldt-schoens" Petrus was an expert. He knew just how to cut and make them as soft, comfortable and silent as Indian moccasins. Many a pair had his uncle and grandfather worn on successful bush-shooting expeditions, where silence and quietness were so essential. From Yettie's and Theunis' little feet up to grandfather's big ones he could fit them all. The whole family really preferred them to the shiny black boots purchased from the trader, which they always felt obliged to wear on high days and holidays—such as their semi-annual trips to the Johannesburg "Nachtmaals." On such important occasions the girls thought the trader's black ones looked more appropriate, with their full bright print skirts and "kappies"—or polk bonnets—which they always wore with heavy veils, to protect their complexions from the hot rays of the African sun.

Meantime Aunt Johanna was directing the Hottentot girls in their task of making the family soap and candles, while Magdalena and her little sisters were out in the kitchen having a great time cooking delicious "Candy-Lakkers." They were expecting company.

By ten o'clock all work was stopped. Every one was tired. So the men's pipes were brought out, with sweet cakes and hot coffee for all. The Boers are such great coffee-drinkers that Aunt Johanna already had plenty of it ready. She kept it hot on her little charcoal stove all day, and served it morning, noon, and night to her family, and often between times, to passing friends.

Unlike Uncle Abraham, who was a typical, tall, spare and straight Boer, with a long beard and grave but kindly face, Aunt Johanna was fair, plump and handsome. She was one of those affectionate, massive, large-hearted Dutch vrouws who are never quite so happy as when entertaining visitors. She loved to bestow upon her friends the best of everything, until "Weltefreden," which sheltered four generations under its broad roof, became known far and wide for its cordial hospitality.

George and his father were among those who called at almost any time. Sometimes the lieutenant came by himself. No one was more welcome. He came often to inquire of Uncle Abraham concerning the work of the skilled inspectors sent out by the "Imperial Land Association" with seeds, implements, and much good advice.

From his room-window, up under the hot galvanized iron roof, Petrus could see through the trees in the distance, the little dorprailroad station, where the trains came puffing in twice a day with the mail. He could hear their whistles as they started out again on their way north to Johannesburg—sometimes bearing thousands of pounds of Marino wool from his uncle's fine flocks to be sold in Johannesburg's great "Market Square" during "Nachtmaal" time, when great crowds of worshipers would be there to exchange their own market produce as well.

Petrus gazed long and silently from his window. His thoughts were following the receding train as it flew on its way to the "GoldenCity," where his Aunt Kotie lived. His face brightened. "In three more years that train will speed on its way from the Cape to Cairo in Egypt! That is over six thousand miles—but I must plan to go! I must save up a great deal of money for such a wonderful trip! Oh, if only I can do it! In three years I shall just be through High School in Johannesburg," thought Petrus joyfully to himself. "But I shall miss seeing George all that time!" This regret was genuine, for Petrus had grown very fond of his little English comrade, who, although nearly the same age, was a full head shorter.

A Cape cart came spinning along the road towards the house. Petrus' dog Hector was barking loudly.

"Oh, there they come now!" exclaimed Petrus. His eyes sparkled as he sprang to the door to give them welcome. But Magdalena had reached the door first and was waiting out on the stoop, where the Englishman's cart had already stopped, and Mutla was busy in-spanning their horses. Petrus and his sister led the way into the house where Aunt Johanna greeted them. She had invited them for dinner. Everybody was glad to see them. Even "Katrina," the large pet baboon, fastened at one side of the entrance, barked a loud "hello" as George passed, and a dear little playful gray monkey on the other side, chattered a friendly greeting as George stopped to give it a pat.

In the central room, which served as drawing-room, music-room and study, the family had gathered to receive their guests. They were seated around in a circle — the women and girls being gorgeously arrayed in pink or green full skirts, tight waists and pearl necklaces. As the lieutenant and George went the rounds shaking hands in accordance with an old Boer custom, each greeted them heartily.

Uncle Abraham and Grandfather Joubert, who had been out in the fields all morning directing the Kafirs, came in hungry for their dinner and glad to see the Wortleys. It was noon-time and the time when the heavy midday meal in all Boer households is served. So Aunt Johanna led the way at once out to the clean, light dining-room, with its spotlessly white walls, where they took their places around the long, family table, standing silently, while Grandfather Joubert read a Psalm from the old, brass-bound Bible. Then Great-grandfather Joubert invoked the blessing with a long grace, to which everybody listened reverently with folded hands — even Petrus and George, who had been allowed places next to each other.

Before Vrouw Joubert the coffee-urn steamed invitingly. She always superintended, and often cooked these meals herself, to which ten or twelve persons usually sat down. As she poured the coffee, several hideous brown-faced Hottentot girls, in bright calico dresses with colored beads and ribbons, silently entered and stood ready to pass the plates. Magdalena served the excellently cooked mutton, vegetables, rice-pudding, fruit, with good wholesome bread just fresh from the oven. Then "konfyt"—a sort of crystallized fruit—was passed to the boys, to spread on their bread and butter.

Everybody ate silently for the most part, as is Boer custom. But Lieutenant Wortley complimented Vrouw Joubert on the excellence of her coffee, and added pleasantly: "Petrus must be getting to be quite a good young farmer-lad by this time, isn't he?"

"The best for his age in the Transvaal!" proudly asserted Uncle Abraham. "He is learning to use the cultivator, and becoming quite an expert at it, too. But I think Petrus likes sheep-farming best, don't you, Koos?"

"Yes, Uncle Abraham, sheep-farming is what I like best. There is no better grazing-lands in all South Africa than the Transvaal has, and I always feel so proud of our great loads of snow-white wool, every bag stamped with 'Weltefreden' in big letters on it, when we send it up for sale at 'Nachtmaal' time. When we go next week, am I not to stay a few days, and visit Aunt Kotie afterwards?"

"Yes, Koos, if you like. My Kafirs are already hard at work shearing the sheep. To-morrow the wool-washing down at the spruitbegins, with the drying and packing after that. Perhaps George would like you to take him down there after dinner to watch the Kafirs at their shearing for a while."

"Yes, thank you," quickly answered the lieutenant for his son. "And George is very curious to see what was left of the devastated mealie-fields since that awful day last spring, if Petrus will be good enough to show him."

"Yes, indeed," agreed Petrus. "I'll have Mutla bring the ponies right after dinner. But, oh, Lieutenant Wortley, I do wish George could go with us up to the Johannesburg 'Nachtmaal,' next week!"

"My dear Petrus, I think George prefers to remain with his father. He has never yet fully recovered from that terrible fright Dirk gave us all last spring," replied the lieutenant with a grave face. "George is truly homesick for England—for our old home in London, and to be with his Aunt Edith again. I am seriously considering disposing of my farm, and returning with my boy, yet not without some regret, for the Transvaal has a bright future."

"Oh, Lieutenant Wortley, please do not take George away! But if you do, and Uncle Abraham will let me, can't I go along to see London? I'd be back here in time for High School. I'll promise that."

Petrus had never seen the ocean, but George had often told him of the great breakers that dash on the rocks at Cape Town, and of the wonderful ocean voyage he had coming from England—of London with its great Westminster Abbey, and busy streets where no dark-hued Zulus went about terrifying everybody brandishing assegais. It had long been Petrus' dream to travel—not only from the "Cape to Cairo" when the new road was done—but to cross the ocean to London.

"Next week, Petrus, George is going with me to Cape Town. We will visit the Government House and see the sights. How would you like to go with us there, Koos?" affectionately replied the lieutenant, who was as fond of Petrus as any Britisher could be of the best of Boer boys.

"Great! I shall be delighted to go along! That will be a splendid trip, and my visit with Aunt Kotie will just be over then. Thank you so much, Lieutenant Wortley."

"It is very kind of you to invite Petrus, Lieutenant," assured Uncle Abraham. "He will have a fine time, and can join you and George at the end of his visit."

The Hottentot girls carried around a towel and basin of water. After each in turn had washed, all stood while Great-grandfather Joubert returned thanks for the food, then withdrew to the music-room to hear Aunt Johanna sing.

"Petrus, come, let's look through the 'far-seer'!" exclaimed George, picking up the telescope, and gazing through the window, towards the extensive orchard of standard peach-trees planted in long rows.

"Aim the 'far-seer' at the Kafir kraals, George. They are away beyond all those tall blue-gum trees—and beyond the mealie-fields, too. You've never seen the way Kafirs live, have you, George? I'll take you over there some day."

But George had turned the telescope onto the near-by trees and bushes, in whose branches and tops there seemed to be literally hundreds of cooing turtle-doves, and somber-hued, scarlet-billed finches, while far over the tops of the highest trees some hawks were silently circling about. Close by, in a pool of water, a number of shy little Hottentot ducks were happily floating around.

"They are different from our English birds," said George. "In England we have robin redbreasts, meadow-larks, swallows and orioles, but our birds do not have such brilliant feathers as these. Oh, I see Mutla with the ponies! Come on, Koos, now let's go!"

"Sh-o-o-o-o-h! Aunt Johanna is playing for us on the organ. She's going to sing. Come, listen!" protested Petrus under his breath. Petrus loved to hear his aunt and cousins sing Psalm-tunes with the organ. He could play many hymns fairly well himself.

While Aunt Johanna sang, Uncle Abraham and Grandfather Joubert got out some big cigars and smoked, as they listened, seated in large comfortable chairs. The girls sat as quiet as mice, applying themselves to their fancy-work and sewing.

Presently Magdalena was asked to play the Volkslied, or national anthem. All stood up and joined heartily in the singing. Petrus and George watched their chance. When Franzina and Yettie began some badly played mazurkas and dance-tunes of their own on the concertina, they quietly slipped out. In a twinkling they were off on their ponies, which Mutla had long had waiting for them at the stoop.

CHAPTER III

A TRANSVAAL "MODEL FARM"

"Whoa, Ferus!

"This won't do, George. It's too hot to gallop like that. Let's go slower." The flaming of the midday sun on the perspiring boys was becoming intolerable.

"I wish I had a pony like Ferus, Koos. He's great!"

"Ferus is a Basuto. They are sure-footed, hardy little beasts for traveling in South Africa. They can travel from five to six miles an hour the live-long day—carrying heavy loads, too—and scarcely feel it. But the Cape ponies are the most wonderful ones for hunting and shooting. They aren't afraid of anything. They are taught to stand still, half a day, sometimes, right where you leave them, by merely turning the bridle over their heads."

"Koos, did you ever go hunting?" asked George. "Daddy says you Boer boys are trained to ride from the time you can walk, and to handle a gun as easily as an English boy does a cane. Is that so?"

"Boer boys are all good marksmen, George. Once I had an older brother David. He was but thirteen—just my age—when the war broke out, and my father, grandfather and great-grandfather all took to horse and gun in defense of their country. You and I were not born then. Young as he was, he shouldered a musket and bravely fought at my father's side until both were killed in the same terrible battle. There was a whole regiment of Boer boys fighting in the war no older than was David. Some were even less. Many were only twelve. And they fought at the side of great-grandfathers of seventy and over. As for big game hunting—I'd like to hear some of your father's exciting experiences hunting in that awful Kalahari Desert, George. Were you with him there long?"

"No, Koos—a very short time. I can't bear to talk about it. I never want to see the place again! That terrible Zulu, Dirk, was there! You ought to see all daddy's trophies—beautiful pelts, Koodoo horns, hides, and ivory from many a fine tusker! Daddy had plenty of big game shooting—lions, elephants and everything! Several times he almost lost his life. But all that was before mother died, and Aunt Edith brought me here to father. But I want to go home."

"But is the Kalahari Desert as bad as people say?"

"Worse! It's just thousands and thousands of miles of burning hot sand. Nothing grows there but a few dried-up low Karroo bushes. My clothes were always all torn up by awful prickly bushes just full of long hack-thorns like fish-hooks."

"'Wacht-een-bigte' is what we Boers call them. It is a kind of cactus, or giraffe-acacia bush. The thorns are exasperating!"

"And the only water one could get was from salty, hot, muddy pools nearly a hundred miles apart. That is why the place is called 'The Great Thirst Land.' Father says, too, that at night the hyenas came so close that once they stole his clothes as he slept."

"W-h-e-w!" exclaimed Koos.

George shuddered, as an ebony-faced black approached them.

"Now, George, don't be afraid. That's only Shobo, the Bushman. There goes your father and Uncle Abraham riding about the farm together. They have stopped away over by the willows, to watch the Kafirs branding cattle. They drive them inside that fence, fasten the gate, then quickly lasso each beast—one by one—by the hind leg, trip it over, and apply the hot iron. It doesn't really hurt them, you know."

"Petrus, what is this we are coming to? Your mealie-fields?"

"The mealie-fields, yes, but there's not a blade of corn. The locusts left all uncle's acres as bare as though burnt by a fire."

"Do tell me about it, Koos. Couldn't you stop them?"

"Nothing could be done. We found the Kafirs from the kraals out in great numbers, galloping their ponies up and down between the long rows of corn, firing their guns, beating on tin cans, yelling and making the most hideous noise and racket, their packs of barking dogs following after them, hoping to scare the locusts away. But they had settled to stay. Oh, George, you just ought to have seen all the Kafir women gathering up the crawling insects—most of them over two inches long—into great heaps, filling every kind of pan and pot, then roasting them over the flames and ravenously devouring them on the spot. The little Bush-children, too, gobbled them up greedily while they were still hot. They considered them great dainties, I'm sure. What they could not eat they carried over to the kraals, where the Kafir women ground them between stones into a sort of meal. They mixed this with grease and fat and baked it into cakes. Even the horses, dogs, cats and chickens gobbled the locusts up with a relish. Look! There goes funny little Shobo, trying to catch a pony for Aunt Johanna's cart. Yes—Shobo's catching him all right."

Before them, as they rode on, stretched miles of Uncle Abraham's richest pasture-lands. Grazing about, in the afternoon sun, were great herds of his uncle's fine horses, sturdy little ponies, mules, sleek herds of fat oxen, and great flocks of sheep and goats.

The contented lowing of the fat cattle, the soft bleating of the sheep and goats, was music in Koos' ears.

"Listen, George, don't you like to hear it?" asked the Boer boy. Like his uncle, Petrus delighted in the beauty and superiority of the farm-beasts, many of which he knew by name. They would come at his call. Petrus loved the vast farm. Even the name—"Weltefreden"—was dear to him.

George gazed about the scene of happy pastoral life before him. His father had often told him of the pleasure the Boers took in the joys of their farm-life. He had heard him say that the Boers' love for their pastoral life makes them believe that the Old Testament is all about themselves. No wonder the daily reading of the Sacred Book meant so much to them! George was beginning to understand what his father meant. Truly, the Boer farmers seemed to be trying to re-live in the Transvaal the ideal life shown them in the pages of Holy Writ. "All those sheep, calves and goats across there are a part of Magdalena's dowry. Magdalena is engaged to be married to the son of the Predikant of our little Dutch Reformed Church—Hercules van der Groot. He asked her for an 'upsit' at once. She will have a fine dowry, for uncle has been giving her part of all the new-born lambs, kids and fowls ever since she was little like Franzina and Yettie. He is doing the same for each of them too."

"And I suppose your uncle will give you a great farm with cattle and beasts of all kinds for your own, some day, and then you will become a rich farmer like he is, and just settle right down here in the Transvaal forever," suggested the English boy.

"'Boer' means 'farmer,' George. That's what we all are—farmers. And do you know what 'Transvaal' means? It means 'across the Vaal River.' And there's no finer land or climate in all South Africa than ours. Many Boer sons do settle down on their fathers' farms forever. Many are born, live and die right here in the Transvaal. Neither my grandfather nor great-grandfather were ever outside of South Africa. They were too busy fighting the natives. Uncle, of course, lost everything in the war. Since then he's had no time for travel. But it's different with me, George. I mean to see something of the world. I'm saving all the money uncle gives me for travel. It's a six thousand mile trip from Cape Town to Cairo. But when the great 'Cape to Cairo' railroad is finished three years from now, George, I'm sure I shall want to go. Maybe I can save money enough. Then I've heard so much about England. I want to visit London, and Westminster Abbey, and see everything."

"Oh, Koos, if ever you do come to London, you must look us up sure. We will be glad to see you."

"Thank you, George. I would not miss seeing you there. There goes 'old Piete'—our Hottentot wagon-driver—with a mule-team load of firewood. And here comes Mutla from the sheep-shearing. I hope the Kafirs are not all through.

"Mutla, what about the sheep-shearing? Is it all over?"

"Yes, my master," answered the Kafir.

"Well, George, I'm sorry we have missed it. Sheep-shearing days are always great days on the farm, when half a hundred Kafirs from the kraals are all working at once. They have been at it all this week. To-morrow the wool-washing and drying begins. Then follows the packing for market. At the last count, uncle's great flock of Merinos numbered six thousand; at least that is the nearest we could come to it, for there are so many that we never can be sure exactly how many the jackals have taken over night. It's fun, though, every morning to try to count them, as they follow each other just as fast as possible, leaping over the gate from the inclosure into the pasture. You ought to see clever little Shobo. Every time he spies a jackal he chases it into a porcupine's hole, only to see it speedily driven out. Suppose we go over towards the Kafir kraals, George? Shall we?"

"Oh, yes, Petrus, let's do!" exclaimed George in delight. They were riding along through the willow, wattle and wild-tobacco trees bordering the pretty little spruit of clear water, where the wool-washing would take place to-morrow.

It was George's first trip to South Africa. He had never seen a Kafir kraal. He had heard that South Africa was a "land of diamonds"; that in "every stone the gold glittered"; that vermillion flamingoes stand on the river-banks gazing down at the little fishes; that gorgeous feathered beauties flit through the African forests, glancing from branch to branch in the bright sunlight but that they had no song; that the Bushman's dogs had no bark; that the flowers were without fragrance; the skies without clouds, and the rivers often without water.

George wondered if he would ever see any of those strange wild animals with unspellable and unpronounceable names about which he had read so much in his African hunting and travel books—Koodoos, gemsbuck, wildebeestes, bushbuck, waterbuck, troops of gnus, with tails like horses, and spiral horns glittering in the sunlight, spotted hyenas, droves of blessbok, tsessebe, and a very strange animal called blaauwbok—whatever that could be.

"Petrus, I wish I could hide in the top of a very high tree and get a good look at a real Tsavo 'man-eater,' and perhaps, just as he wasabout to spring, a little Bushman, with nothing but his poisoned arrows, would come out and kill him."

"I can't promise you'll see any terrible 'man-eaters,' George, but you'll soon see a Bushman or two, perhaps half a hundred black Kafirs, and maybe a—"

"Zulu?" broke in George. "Petrus, I'm going home. See those black clouds coming? It will rain soon."

"Not a single Zulu! I'll promise you that, George. Uncle has not one on the place. Mutla has strict orders to keep them away. The Kafirs are perfectly harmless. They're a good-natured crowd of fellows. You will like them. They are not real savages, George. Many of them are intelligent and anxious for education. Some of the best study in the negro schools of the United States. But most of them still live with their dogs, chickens, goats and other animals all mixed up together in their kraals. The 'Red Kafirs,' off in Bondoland, and the Transkei, on the coast, still mix red clay into their hair and cover their bodies with it."

"I'd rather face all the Kafirs in Kaffraria than one Zulu, Petrus!" protested George. "I'm never afraid of Mutla."

"Wait until you see some of the happy-faced, laughing Zulus of Natal—the Durban 'ginrickshaw' Zulu boys for instance. You will never be afraid of them. Zulus are not all dangerous—like Dirk. Many of them make good, honest house-servants, and are to be trusted. Kafirs work better in the fields. Fine specimens as many of them are, yet the best of them are not the equals of the magnificent big Zulus of Natal and Zululand—splendidly built, coal-black giants like Dirk."

"Petrus, here come two Kafirs now!" whispered George.

"Those are Hottentots, George," laughed Petrus. "Don't you see their tufty hair—all little wiry balls with open spaces between, just like the Bushman's. Both are little yellow-brown, flat-faced people who click, click, when they try to talk. The word 'Hottentot' means a 'Stammerer' or 'Jabberer.' We cannot understand their jargon, and Uncle Abraham and I have to talk to them by signs. The Kafirs scorn the Hottentots, and the Hottentots hate the pigmy Bushmen. They won't work together. There goes a little Bushman, now. They have no lobes to their ears. Many of them sleep out in the open—winter and summer. On cold nights they sometimes lie so close to the fire that they blister their bodies until the skin peels off. But they are great little hunters. They always know where to find water. They will watch the flight of the birds, or spoor some animal to his drinking-place, and when on the hunt they'll eat the flesh of anything, from an elephant to a mouse."

"Ugh! Snakes, too, Koos?"

"Yes. Snakes, lizards, tortoises, grubs, frogs, locusts, flying ants, ostrich eggs, wild honey, young bees, nestling birds of all kinds, and all sorts of bulbs and roots they dig up with pointed sticks. And you know how their arrowheads are always smeared with poison."

"Ugh! Bushmen must be disgusting! No wonder the Kafirs hate them. I should, too!" protested George. "Look! Petrus, we've reached the Kafir kraals!"

Spread out before them, just beyond a few tall trees, were twenty or more odd-looking huts, arranged in a semicircle. They could see the naked little black children playing about and hear their chatter. Beautiful herds of fat cattle, guarded by huge, dark-hued Kafirs, came slowly winding along the road past them, on their way to the cattle-kraals for their evening milking. It was almost sunset.

"Petrus, see those black clouds! It's going to rain!"

There came a loud clap of thunder. Mutla galloped quickly across to Petrus. Springing lightly to the ground, he exclaimed:

"Oh, my master, come quick to kraals! Rain, bad rain!"

"You are right, Mutla. George, come quick! We must hurry home! We are in for a drenching!"

They put their ponies to the gallop and scampered over the soaking ground as another crash of thunder brought the water down in sheets.

It was one of those frequent, heavy, sub-tropical downpours which come and go so quickly in the southern hemisphere.

CHAPTER IV

THE GREAT "TREK"

Great-grandfather Joubert was a very patriarch in years. A full century had passed over his head. They had all been such active years, full of stirring memories. Through his rugged features there shone the same big-hearted kindliness which had marked all his days.

Petrus loved him. No one could tell quite such fascinating tales as he; thrilling tales of early adventure and conquests; of hair-breadth escapes from wild animals and savage natives in the final conquering of the African Veldt; tales of the terrible "Border Wars," and of long wars against the British.

To Great-grandfather Joubert his country's history was sacred history. It had all taken place before his very eyes. In fact, he had helped to make it. Even in his eighty-fifth year he had scaled the Transvaal hills and done scouting duty with all but the agility of his sons, grandsons, and great-grandsons fighting bravely at his side.

He often sat thinking it over. Few of the old "Voor-trekker" Boers were still living—those who had "trekked" in their great ox-wagons across the deadly "Karroo," finally to settle in the Transvaal. But that great "Exodus"—known in Boer history as the "Great Trek of 1836"—was one of Great-grandfather Joubert's most vivid memories. He was but a boy then.

The mid-summer heat was so oppressive that Great-grandfather Joubert had asked to have his comfortable armchair moved over close by the open window, just above the syringa bush. He liked the scent.

But two weeks now remained until Christmas time—about the hottest season of the year in South Africa. In another week would come the yearly festival commemorating that tragic episode of December 16, 1836, "Dangaan's Daag," when the immortal Piet Retief, with a number of the Voor-trekkers, left the main party and made their way down into Natal, only to be massacred by the Zulus.

All day long Great-grandfather Joubert sat there beside the open window smoking his ornate pipe filled with fragrant tobacco and reading from the large, silver-bound Bible on his knees, whose open pages were swept by his long, grizzly beard. He was a typical "Takhaar" Boer.

Aunt Johanna had brought him the Sacred Book, with some hot coffee and rolls. From the window he could see Uncle Abraham riding about the farm to see that his beasts were all right, counting his flocks, and superintending his Kafirs.

The Hottentot maids fetched him his dinner. Then Petrus brought him the latest Johannesburg and London daily newspapers. He often sat and read to him carefully everything of interest—especially the latest "war-news"—which filled all the leading pages, nowadays, with accounts of the terrible "world-war" raging throughout Europe between Germany and the Allies. Thus Great Britain—their mother-country—had been plunged into the fearful conflict. Great-grandfather Joubert wished he was younger that he might go himself to fight for his king. "Race-hatred" had no place in his feelings. The Jouberts belonged to the more intelligent, unprejudiced class of Boers who had long ceased to regard the British as intruders. He had always believed with Paul Kruger—the great Boer leader of his day—that "Where love dwells prosperity follows."

As he re-read the old story of the wanderings of the Israelites in the Wilderness—they scarcely knew whither—the trials and hardships they had encountered—it seemed to him that the Sacred Book was telling the story of the "Great Trek" of his own people. The Boers, too, had wandered forth—had suffered hardship and injustice no less than had the patriarchs of old—he told himself. Closing the book, he folded his hands, and, leaning comfortably back in his armchair, he gazed far across the grassy sweep of high veldt, with its red-brown scattered kopjes, towards the western horizon. Soon he was lost in the memories of a century.

Softly the room door opened. In a twinkling Petrus' arms were flung around the old man's neck.

"A penny for your thoughts, Grandfather dear! Please let me stay here with you a while," begged the boy.

"Ah, Koos, is it you, my boy? Yes, yes, you may stay a while if you do not ask too many questions. It is easy to guess your thoughts. Let me try. Your visit with Aunt Kotie at Johannesburg next week. Your trip to Cape Town with Lieutenant Wortley and George. Hurrying back home in time for Christmas. Isn't that right, Koos?"

"Yes, Grandfather, and George is expecting a big Christmas box from his Aunt Edith in England. Now for yours!"

"I should have to take you back to the early days in the Old Colony, Koos, when I was but a boy like yourself. And, like you, I used to beg my old grandfather for 'stories' of his country, which was France. He was one of several hundred French Huguenots who fled from their own country to South Africa, because they could not worship as they liked. Those were happy days in the Old Colony there on our large, quiet farms, before British rule became intolerable. Our people were prosperous slave-holders. My father owned as many as eighty Hottentots. But as British oppression became more and more intolerable—our slaves liberated, and indignities of every kind heaped upon us—our Boer leaders resolved to endure no more and the great 'Exodus'—known in history as the 'Great Trek of 1836'—began. I shall never forget those awful days. I was just a boy then."

"Why didn't the Boers rebel?" indignantly questioned Petrus.

"Rebellion was useless. But we knew of a vast land that stretched away to the north of us. To be sure, it was filled with savages and ferocious wild animals, but even that was preferable to British tyranny. There were about six thousand of us in all who left our fertile coastland farms and trekked forth into the unknown wilderness in search of new homes where we could live in peace. One by one, we loaded up our huge ox-drawn wagons, which were to serve as home, fort and wagon for many a long day on our journey. Inside these great covered wagons—'rolling-houses'—the Zulus called them—the women and children were seated. Outside—tramping alongside as a guard—carrying their well-oiled, long-barreled guns—were the men. The older children helped to drive and round up the great flocks and herds which accompanied our migration. Well do I remember the cries of a small, bare-foot boy of ten, running at the head of a long team of tired oxen, which now and then quickened its pace at the touch of his sjambok. Who do you suppose that bit of a boy was, Koos?"

"You, Grandfather?"

"No, no, Koos. That little fellow was only about half my size then, but, since those hard days, he has four times ruled our glorious Transvaal as its President, and often fought with us all for our country's freedom."

"Oh, I know! President Kruger?"

"Yes, Koos, that ragged little boy was none other than Paul Stephanus Kruger."

"Go on, Grandfather. Did the Voor-trekkers come straight to the Transvaal with all their covered ox-wagons and everything?"

"No, Koos. There were the great desolate stretches of the 'Karroo' to be crossed, with such dangers and hardships by day and night that many of our oxen soon trekked their last trek. The loud gun-like crack of the long ox-whips, as they whirled over the poor oxen's heads—and fell with a savage blow on their brown hides—to the driver's yell: "!—is still in my ears. Those whips, made from the hide of giraffes, were usually eighteen or twenty feet long.

"This great 'Exodus'—or 'the Boer Mayflower trip'—as your cousins in New York City once described it—was full of all kinds of experiences and suffering. Vast herds of wild elephants impeded our way. Flocks of ostriches, with herds of zebras, antelopes, gnus and quaggas, covered the plains in such vast numbers that at times the whole landscape was obscured. Poisonous snakes glided from among the bushes in front of us— and there was scarcely a rocky kloof or kopje but sheltered a ravenous lion or leopard."

"Oh, Grandfather! and were your dangers over when you'd crossed that terrible Karroo?"

"No, Koos, they were just beginning. All the Voor-trekkers did not go in one direction. They spread out like a fan from the Mother Colony, advancing by different routes. About two hundred followed Hendrik

Potgieter to the banks of the Vaal, into the land we now call the Orange Free State. Another small party trekked its way down to Delegoa Bay where all but two perished from the horrible poisonous marshes. I was with the main party, which continued on farther northward, and finally settled here in the Transvaal. Here we encounteredthe fierce Matebele, who attacked us in large numbers. Quickly we chained our wagons together into a huge circle—making a 'lagger' or fort of them, and fired on the savages from that ambuscade—our women bravely loading and re-loading our guns for us. They rushed madly upon us and fought like demons— stabbing in through the spokes of the wheels. Desperate as we were, Boers are good marksmen, and finally the Matebele were driven off, but not until many of our brave people were massacred, and six thousand head of our cattle and sheep taken. Then we had fifty years of terrible Kafir wars—Zulu wars—and Border Wars of the most horrible kind against the savage natives before we could possess the land—our own Transvaal—in peace."

"Oh, Grandfather! Grandfather! I'm so glad your life was spared!" cried Petrus, flinging his arms tightly about his great-grandfather's neck. "But you forgot to tell me the story of 'Dangaan's Daag' and Piet Retief." Petrus never tired of hearing of that famous march of the Voor-trekkers to Natal under their heroic leader, Piet Retief. History tells us it was comparable only to the march of the Greek Ten Thousand in Asia.

"No, Koos, I've told you that story a hundred times. I'm thankful I did not join that fatal party. One of your uncles went."

"Was it Uncle Petrus Jacobus, Grandfather? The one who was made President next after Kruger, and who became a famous general? The one who was made commander-in-chief of all the Boer forces, and gained the victories of Majuba Hill and Laing's Neck, against the British? The uncle whose name I bear? Oh, Grandfather, may I see his picture? The one in your old iron chest?" begged Petrus excitedly.

"Here is the key, Koos. Lift out the things. It is in an old portfolio down in the very bottom."

One by one, Petrus spread the precious keepsakes from the Boer war on the floor about the old chest. It was a strange collection. The first thing his hand touched, was an old "bandoler"—or cartridge-belt—heavy with unspent cartridges—now green with mold. Petrus laid it on the floor at his great-grandfather's feet. Next came a long-barreled, old gun—the sight of which made Koos' eyes sparkle with interest, but a tear fell down the old Boer's bronzed cheek as he lifted the rusty Mauser and read the words cut on its stock thirteen years ago: "For God, Country, and Justice." Silently he examined it, but Koos could read in his flashing eyes that he was hearing again the distant rolling of artillery, the crackling of rifles, the shrieking of shells through the air—made bright by the sweeping searchlights of the enemy. Then Petrus lifted out an old broad-brimmed slouch hat. Embroidered on the band around its crown were the words: "For God and Freedom," and sewed on one side of the upturned brim was a rosette of the "Vier-kleur," and the fluffy brown tail of a meerscat. A small roll containing a blanket and a mackintosh came next.

"Grandfather, I don't see the portfolio," protested Koos, who had about reached the bottom of the old chest.

"Go on, Koos, you will find it along with my old Bible—the one I read between battles."

Carefully Petrus lifted out a great silken flag and unfurled it—its bright horizontal stripes of red, white and blue, being crossed by a band of green—the "Vier-kleur" of the Republic. Within the folds of the old flag he had found a well-worn pocket Bible and the portfolio.

"Hand me the flag, too, Koos," said the old man. He touched its silken folds tenderly—almost with affection. "This flag belonged to the days before the annexation of the Transvaal to Great Britain—before our present 'Union of South Africa' existed. Its colors tell of the time when the Transvaal was the 'South African Republic,' Koos."

"Shall we always have to fly the 'Union Jack' in the Transvaal, Grandfather? George says it helps him to feel more at home down here."

"It may be God's will, Petrus. Let us hope that the worst of our troubles are forever over. During the thirteen years since peace was signed between Great Britain and the Transvaal our friendly relations have been deepening. A new era of progress, prosperity and peace seems to have come for the Transvaal. Our future looks bright."

"The portfolio, Grandfather? Is Uncle Petrus' picture there? And tell me all about his great victories of Majuba Hill and Laing's Neck, won't you? I've never heard enough about them."

"I can't talk of those days, Koos. Divine favor guided our footsteps, and, victories though they were, those days cost us many of our best-loved kinsfolk—even your little thirteen-year-old cousin Martinus, who fought so bravely in the 'Penkop Regiment'—a whole regiment made up of school-children like himself. There were also great-grandfathers like myself. Paul Kruger was seventy-five, and hundreds of his gray-haired burghers fighting with him were even older. Your Uncle Petrus, when in command of all the Boer forces, was very close to seventy.

"We never wanted to fight and kill our fellow-beings. It was heart-rending to us," continued the aged man, vehemently, as he handed Petrus the picture of General Joubert. "All we asked for was peace to cultivate the soil, and worship together. But every burgher in the Transvaal—from President Kruger and your Uncle Petrus down to little Martinus—swore to yield his life's blood rather than fail to defend his country's right to freedom. For that their fathers had suffered and died."

"I've heard Uncle Abraham say that it was just a 'Wait-a-bit' peace the Boers signed in 1902, Grandfather. Do you think so?"

"No, Petrus. Loyalty to the mother country is deepening in the Transvaal every day. Premier Botha and all his people are ready to fight in her behalf at any time. Now run along. There comes George galloping across to see you, Koos. I'll put these things back in the chest myself."

"Thank you, Grandfather dear, for all you've told me," called back Petrus, as he bounded downstairs to meet George, who had come to take part in the short twilight games of the early tropical evening which Petrus,

Franzina, Yettie and Theunis always played together just before dinner-time.

Scarcely had darkness given place to a bright moonlight than Magdalena's favorite "freyer" — Hercules van der Groot — came riding over on his "kop-spuiling" courting horse — tossing his head, prancing and jumping all the way (being sharply bitted and curbed for the purpose). As Hercules always liked to look very imposing on these important courting occasions he had decked himself out in a fine yellow cord jacket, vest and trousers, changed his veldt-schoens for a pair of shiny tight patent-leather congress gaiters, above which he wore a pair of showy leather leggings. Waving gracefully in the breeze from one side of his broad-brimmed white felt slouch hat was a tall ostrich plume — and in his pocket he had not forgotten to place a nice box of "Dutch Mottoes." He had ridden twenty miles from his father's farm Vergelegen.

Upon Aunt Johanna's inviting him to enter, he politely shook hands with each member of the family, then seated himself in a corner against the wall, patiently waiting for an opportunity to speak alone with Magdalena, when he quickly whispered in her ear: "We'll set oop this necht."

Finally, after the family had retired, Magdalena appeared dressed in a pink dress with bright ribbons of every shade, and much jewelry encircling her neck. In one hand she carried a match box and in the other a piece of candle, which — to Hercules' delight — he noticed was a long one. According to rigid Boer etiquette he must depart when the candle had burned out. Together they lighted the taper and placed it upon the table alongside the plate of "Candy Lakkers" which Magdalena had that morning made especially for her freyer, who produced his "Dutch Mottoes." As Hercules kept an eye on the diminishing candle, anxiously guarding it from drafts, seeing to it that it should not flit or flare, and trimming it from time to time, he told her how much he admired her uncle's new horses, how well the oxen looked after the rain, and other such interesting things — not forgetting to assure her that he loved her very much. But as time flies with lovers so with lights, and the interview was abruptly terminated, but not before it was agreed they should be married on New Year's Day, and that their honeymoon trip should be to the Victoria Falls on the Zambesi.

CHAPTER V

A BOER "NACHTMAAL"

For two days Johannesburg's great "Market Square" had been filled with out-spanned heavy ox-drawn wagons. Uncle Abraham and Petrus had arrived with hundreds of other Boer farmers from the surrounding country, for the semi-annual "Nachtmaal"—which really means "night meal" or "Sacrament." It was always an occasion of great excitement and bustle. For, besides the "Divine Service," which lasted all day, there was the pleasurable excitement of meeting old friends, making new ones, shopping, selling, and putting through of business deals. Most of the burghers brought their whole families with them. But Uncle Abraham and Petrus had had to come alone this year. Great-grandfather Joubert was not very well. They greatly missed Aunt Johanna, Magdalena and the children.

Aunt Kotie had urged them to stay with her. But because of the big load of wool he had to sell, Uncle Abraham thought it best to remain in the "Market Square" where all the transactions were made.

To the Boer youths and maidens "Nachtmaal" meant a time of baptisms, confirmations, engagements, and marriages. After the services of the day were over, Boer sweethearts met under the blinking stars in the shadow of the tent-wagons and repeated love's old story to each other.

Half way to Johannesburg they had halted their wagon at a little "Negotic Winkel," or store, to lay in a good supply of sweets—"Lakkers" and "Mottoes"—of which both Uncle Abraham and Petrus were inordinately fond. As they had decided to eat alongside their wagon they purchased also numerous boxes of sardines and sweet biscuits. Coffee they had brought from home.

The first "Divine Service" began at seven o'clock in the morning. The last was not over until long after dark. Before each service—if there was no business to be transacted—the men lingered about the church door discussing their crops, the latest hail storm or drought, their children and their troubles with their Kafirs. The women and girls gathered in chattering groups about the tent-wagons, in their stiff, new print dresses and heavily piped black "kappies" — well-lined and frilled, for the sake of protecting their complexions from the strong African sun.

At the first peal of the organ all trooped into the church, the "Kirkraad" — dressed in black with white neckties — entering first, with the minister, or Predikant, and seating themselves up in the front pews before the pulpit. Then the solemn rites began.

During the brief spaces between services Uncle Abraham and Petrus visited the various stores, carefully attending to the half-yearly shopping for Aunt Johanna. Uncle Abraham also disposed advantageously of his farm produce. He had never brought to market a better clip of wool than this. For it he had just received the very satisfactory price of three hundred golden sovereigns. Of this he had immediately paid out one hundred and fifty pounds in necessary household and agricultural purchases, such as a new cultivator, coffee to last until the next "Nachtmaal," barbed-wire and a large supply of strong, new wool-sacks. He was sorry to be deprived of Aunt Johanna's help.

But together he and Petrus made their purchases, always hurrying instantly back to their pew in the church at the first sound of the bell from the little "bell-tent." As, one by one, the items on the long list were purchased and crossed off, the home-load in the big wagon mounted higher and still higher, until by evening it would hold no more.

It had been a good "Nachtmaal." The inspiring services, old friendships renewed, the large number of marriages and engagements, and the golden sovereigns in his pocket, all told him so. He handed Petrus a generous amount, telling him he might need it on his trip. The sun was sinking in the west, and the trek back to the farm a long one. So he in-spanned his long team of oxen just as Aunt Kotie's motor came whizzing up for Petrus. The boy hesitated. It was his first trip away from home alone. He had never been parted from his dear Uncle Abraham.

As he jumped into her car he could see through the gathering dusk many fathers of families, Bible in hand, standing in their wagons conducting evening service. Aunt Kotie's driver was a Zulu, he noticed, but not with alarm.

"Trek!" yelled Uncle Abraham to his oxen. Aunt Kotie had just promised him she would go with Koos to Kimberley and put him safely in Lieutenant Wortley's care. Petrus waved "good-by" as the big wagon rolled off and vanished in the deepening twilight.

Aunt Kotie lived in Parktown, the most fashionable quarter of the great metropolis. Next morning, from her upper veranda, Petrus got a wonderful bird's-eye view over the city, and off to the Mageliesberg Mountains. South of the city, as Aunt Kotie explained, the Vaal and other streams of the Orange River glided through gorges to the Atlantic Ocean, while northward they flowed to the Limpopo, and then on into the Indian Ocean.

Petrus noticed that a huge, black-skinned Zulu, who eyed him narrowly from time to time, served them at breakfast, and that still another black giant—a particularly evil-looking fellow, under whose tread the very earth shook—helped him and his aunt into the waiting motor car for their sightseeing ride. Aunt Kotie explained that native boys did all her work. She found them more reliable than white help.

As they drove down broad streets, past great stone and marble buildings, palatial club-houses, fine churches, museums, and the High School, Aunt Kotie saw that something was wrong. The people walked briskly and excitedly about the streets. Ugly rumors of anti-German riots had reached her. "Market Square," of yesterday's peaceful "Nachtmaal" was now filled with striking miners, who were in open revolt, she was told, having already attacked and battered in the offices of the Rand gold mines.

So Aunt Kotie ordered her Zulu driver to keep far away from the "Market Square," and instead of visiting the gold-fields they would motor up to Pretoria and back—the Union's capital city, which would be sure to interest Petrus.

In fact, Petrus was having his first glimpse of a great city. Johannesburg was the equal of any great metropolis of Europe, Aunt Kotie told him. It was the wonderful "Golden City" he had long wished to see. He had never been beyond the "Market Square" before. The "City of Midas," it had been called since the discovery of the famous "Witwatersrand" or "White Water's Ridge" south of the city.

As they sped in the direction of Pretoria, Petrus gained a panoramic view of gold mine after mine, from which fabulous wealth had been dug. Vast reservoirs, then mills, with a long row of great iron chimneys came in sight, and the roar of batteries crushing the quartz containing the gold reached their ears.

"These mines must be as rich as the Klondike, Aunt Kotie?" questioned Petrus.

"Hundreds of times as rich. And we are told that buried beneath Johannesburg still lies more gold than the world ever saw."

As their motor entered Pretoria's "Market Square" the band was playing to a gathering of the townsfolk. They could not pause to listen. It was nearly evening, barely time in which to give Petrus a hasty glimpse of the Capital's streets, and especially of the "Kantoors," the government offices for the Union of South Africa, of which General Botha had long been "Premier."

Before leaving Pretoria Aunt Kotie declared that Petrus must see Paul Kruger's old home, if only for one glance. It was a long, low one-story cottage, half-hidden by the roadside trees and shrubbery. Marble lions guarded either side of the entrance to the broad, shady stoop, where on many an afternoon President Kruger had enjoyed his coffee and smoked with his burghers.

"'Oom Paul' his people called him. Every Boer loved him. He was the close friend of your uncle, General Joubert, who commanded the Boer forces, and, of course, your father, grandfather, great-grandfather and Uncle Abraham, all knew him well," explained Aunt Kotie. "Now for home. To-morrow there'll be more sightseeing for you, Koos," added his aunt, who was becoming very fond of her bright young nephew from "Weltefreden."

CHAPTER VI

OVER THE "GREAT KARROO" TO CAPE TOWN

A fearful dust-storm was raging over the Kimberley veldt. Gusts of sand and dirt blew into their faces as Aunt Kotie kissed Petrus good-by. He had just promised to spend his winter at High School in Johannesburg with her. Lieutenant Wortley and George were glad to see their little Boer friend again, but they feared a violent thunderstorm and drenching. The wind was unroofing houses, blowing down trees, and filling the air with rubbish and dirt at a terrific rate.

So the lieutenant hailed an old vehicle. There was just time between trains for a glance at the famous Kimberley diamond mines, which Petrus had never seen. The wheels of the old vehicle often sank a foot deep as it rattled along through clouds of dust, past miserable corrugated-iron shanties and mounds of débris, left after the diamonds had been sorted out. Kimberley seemed to lie in a sea of sand.

To Petrus, the mine looked like a great human ant-hill whose inhabitants were all surging busily about at hard work. They paused at the brink of the gigantic caldron-like hole to take a look far down at the hundreds of naked Kafirs whose bodies looked no larger than rabbits. A man approached and asked if they would not like to be taken down. So they jumped into a hoist, from which a bucket of the precious "blue-stone" had just been discharged, and soon found themselves at the bottom of the vast crater. It was a wonderful sight. There it was that the most beautiful gems in all the world were found!

Hundreds of demon-like figures, hard at work, were emerging from the earth and reëntering it on all sides. They were chiefly Kafirs.

"Oh, I wonder which one of these wretched-looking Kafirs is Mutla's poor, sick brother, Diza!" exclaimed Petrus. "Mutla told me he is afraid Diza will die if he doesn't get away from this underground work here. If only he had the money he said he could get farm work in Rhodesia. I heard the Predikant of uncle's church say there were continual deaths among these wretched Kimberley mine boys who cannot get away," continued Petrus, anxiously scanning the black faces for one that might resemble Mutla's.

The boys hoped to catch a glimpse of a diamond. The ground had all been squared off into different claims—which had cut it up into blocks, cubes and rectangles. Each claim had its own wires and trollies bringing up the precious "blue" to the surface. As the countless tubes of the aerial tramway glided rapidly back and forth—upwards and downwards through the labyrinthine network of wire-rope stretching over the sides of the mine— the vast abyss seemed filled with flights of birds fluttering to and fro.

"Uncle Abraham told me the story about the finding of the first rough gem here," said Petrus to George. "The children of a Dutch farmer had a small soapy-appearing stone for a plaything. They thought it was nothing but a pebble. But a visitor noticed the strange stone one day and offered to buy it. The mother laughed and gave it to him gladly. Then it was examined by many experts and pronounced a valuable diamond."

"That was the beginning of one of the greatest industries the world has ever known," added the lieutenant. "Then from the 'Premier Mine,' near Pretoria, was taken the great 'Cullinan diamond,' which weighed a pound and a half. That was the most valuable diamond ever found, its value being $2,500,000."

"And it was called the 'Star of Africa,' and presented to King Edward, wasn't it, Daddy?" exclaimed George.

"Yes, George. And part of it is set in His Majesty's scepter and part in his crown," explained the lieutenant, as they were bobbing along in the same old vehicle through the sand and dirt and wind-storm for their train. Soon they were whirling towards Cape Town.

For nearly two nights and days the train continued on its way over vast stretches of arid plains. Only a few small, dried-up, lavender-colored "Karroo" bushes here and there were seen, with now and then a flat-topped kopje. They were crossing the "Great Karroo"—a region of limitless sky and sand. Desolation marked every mile of the way.

"It's just like that Kalahari Desert, Father! Some of it has gotten inside this car, too!" protested George. A fine white alkaline powder had penetrated the car, sifted into their baggage, down their collars, into their eyes, hair, and everywhere it should not be. Even the food tasted gritty. All the next day they were still passing over the same great burning waste of sandy, sun-swept veldt. "'Karroo' is a Hottentot name, meaning dry or barren," Petrus explained. Even the river-beds were dried up. Towards evening, when a sudden hard rain fell over the dry tussocky grass, the effect was magical. Hundreds of wild flowers burst suddenly into bloom, glowing brightly in the wilderness.

The boys' excitement in watching for the possible appearance of elephants and giraffes on the "Karroo" was giving way to doubt as none appeared. Petrus had read of as many as five hundred giraffes in one herd.

"All that, Petrus, was before the natives were given fire-arms," explained the lieutenant. "They were allowed to kill most of them off, but there are still plenty of leopards and hyenas left."

"I've heard you say, Daddy, that before Livingstone came and civilized the natives, white people scarcely dared live in Africa at all," interrupted George. "Then, after he taught them and doctored and protected and helped them, they called him 'Messenger of God.'"

"Yes, before Livingstone the Englishmen believed that Africa was a place little better than the Kalahari Desert, with its villainous salt water," declared the lieutenant, with a scowl at the memory.

"Oh, Lieutenant Wortley! One of Aunt Kotie's Zulus looked exactly like that Zulu who threw his assegai at our cart that day. He eyed me closely every minute. I believe he is that very one!" excitedly exclaimed Petrus. "Aunt Kotie said he'd not been with her long."

"Dirk? He'd better keep his distance from George and me if he knows what is good for him!" said the lieutenant, with a threatening look.

"Yes, Dirk! That's just what Aunt Kotie called him. I wish he'd go back to Zululand or the Kalahari Desert and stay there forever!" exclaimed Petrus. The view was fast changing from the "Karroo" and becoming more rugged.

The train curved in and out of the narrowing valleys and zigzagged up and down between beautiful ravines and rugged kloofs. Soon the lofty cathedral-like jagged peaks of the Hottentot's Holland Mountains came in view. Before the boys scarcely knew it they had reached Cape Town and were rushing through the city's streets in a tram for their hotel.

"Oh!" exclaimed both boys at once, as they caught a fine view of towering "Table Mountain." They wanted to go at once down to the dock where they could get a better view of it, but the lieutenant said they must have something to eat first and rest a bit.

"But we are not tired!" protested the boys, as soon as they had eaten a slight meal. So their sightseeing commenced at once. Thestreets of the Colonial metropolis were thronged with a strange medley of busy humanity. Ladies in carriages bent on shopping, Europeans in white suits, turbaned Malay priests in gorgeous silken robes, and British officers and soldiers from the barracks—everywhere. There had been violent anti-German riots, so that now strong forces of police, soldiers, and fire brigades were all being held in readiness to stop further disturbances. General Botha had issued a message of protest.

After the lieutenant had taken George and Petrus down Adderly Street—the Broadway of Cape Town—and shown them the Parliament and Government Houses, the Fine Arts Gallery and the South African College, where Koos expected some day to study, the boys begged to be taken down to the dock.

The Malay driver of a passing hansom cab soon left them at the dock, where they found a strange and motley crowd of shabbily dressed Kafirs, sea-faring men, scantily clad Kroomen from the coast, Russians, Greeks, Italians, Dutch and Polish Jews—all coming and going, with here and there Malays, whose wooden sandals with their strange toe posts, made a clattering noise as they walked.

Beneath the towering granite wall of "Table Mountain"—with its summit enveloped in a perpetual cloud-mist—lay "Table Bay," whose cobalt-blue waters looked smooth as glass—save for the long curving line of tidal ripples where the water and yellow sand met. A swarm of drowsy sea-fowl lightly rose at the approach of a ship. The thought thrilled Petrus. He was enjoying his first glimpse of the ocean.

"This is one of the most beautiful ports in the world," said the lieutenant, as he hailed a passing motor for a drive along the famous "Kloof Road." Soon they were passing through Cape Town's beautiful and picturesque suburbs with its villas half-buried in sub-tropical foliage. Although there remained but a few days until Christmas, flowers were blooming everywhere, roses, purple-blossomed "kafirboom," in airy sprays, spiky aloes with their blood-red flowers, lobelias, and the lovely "Lily of the Nile" which bloomed the year round.

Barely time remained for a quick run out to see "Groote Schuur," the fine old home of Cecil Rhodes—a handsome, low, gabled residence, with an avenue of towering pines leading up to it.

"And was Rhodes buried, like Livingstone, in Westminster Abbey?" asked George.

"No," replied his father. "He was buried on the summit of a lonely mountain in the heart of the great land he developed for England—Rhodesia. His tomb, which was cut out of the native rock, lies in a spot full of grandeur, which he loved and called: 'The View of the World.' A part of his dream for the development of Africa was the vast scheme, now nearing completion, of the 'Cape to Cairo' railroad—a great British stretch of steel from Cape Town to the Mediterranean. People laughed at the wild project of a railway that should run through the entire length of the African continent. Much of the route—all that part in the region of the Equator—would pass through territory inhabited by wild and war-like native tribes, and jungles infested by lions and other wild beasts. But Rhodes toiled away at his vast undertaking until to-day its completion is a matter of but a few more years."

As they passed Newlands, at the foot of the mountain, Petrus and George noticed many picnickers and gay coaching parties "too-tooing" along the beautiful "Kloof Road." Farther on, a lively game of cricket was being played by fine athletic-looking British and South African boys side by side, and there were Malays, in red fezzes and gorgeously colored blazers, playing an interesting game of golf.

Petrus' one beautiful day of sightseeing in Cape Town was about over. Already darkness was fast settling over "Table Mountain" and the city below it, as the little party returned to their hotel through the business streets of the city, which they found thronged with the troops, police, and immense crowds which had gathered in a rather threatening spirit, and were singing, as with one voice, "Rule Britannia." In large headlines all the evening papers told Cape Town's citizens the startling news that one more great power had gone mad and thrown herself into the fearful "world-war."

CHAPTER VII

A KAFIR PARTY AT THE CHIEF'S KRAAL

It was Christmas Day. In the ideal mid-summer weather, neighbors and relatives rode over in groups all morning, until the farmhouse gathering at "Weltefreden" was a large one by the time Petrus reached home. Aunt Johanna had lengthened the tables until thirty were seated for the big Christmas dinner, which she and Magdalena together had prepared. The genuine spirit of hospitality was felt by all. Songs by Aunt Johanna herself, splendid stories by Uncle Abraham, with recitations and organ-playing by the children had followed.

There was to be a dance in the evening in honor of Magdalena and Hercules, and "cross-country" riding parties had been formed forthe afternoon. Aunt Johanna's gift of gracious hospitality always made Christmas and New Year's Day rare occasions, long to be remembered.

Over at Lieutenant Wortley's a surprise awaited George. With his "Christmas box" from England had come his beloved Aunt Edith herself. She could only remain until New Year's Day, but for George's sake she had taken the long trip to South Africa. It was George's first Christmas without his dear mother. Aunt Edith was afraid he would be homesick. As the "tree" was to be a large one, with a dance, and presents for all, she told George he might invite all his little friends from Johannesburg and the surrounding farms.

Of course Petrus promised heartily to be there, then added over the telephone—Boer children and grown-ups, too, can now "call up" their friends on the telephone just as do our American boys and girls—"come over this afternoon, George, can't you? Uncle Abraham promised that I should go to the Kafir children's party—if only for a few minutes. The Chief's giving the party himself. He always gives his people an 'ox-roasting,' you know, on New Year's Day. It's their 'Ancestral Meat Feast.' This year, because of Magdalena's wedding, Uncle Abraham promised him three oxen with which to celebrate. Perhaps that is why he has invited me to their party. Anyway, I shan't enjoy it without you, George. Will you come?"

There was a pause. "Aunt Edith says I can go, Koos, if I'm sure to be back home here before dark — before supper-time. She'll be worried if I'm not. Are you ready to start now?"

"Yes, George. Ride over on your pony. I'll be waiting for you at the front stoop on Ferus."

"All right, Petrus," came George's hearty reply, and by the time Petrus had Ferus up-saddled, George had arrived, and together they started to the kraals, passing on the way gay parties of Magdalena's friends at the tennis courts, and others on the croquet lawns, enjoying themselves in the shade from the orchard trees.

As the Kafir party was to be a very special occasion, with over a hundred little black children present, elaborate preparations for several days past had been under way at the Chief's kraal. The older girls had made fine bead-work, grass and copper-wire bangles for their wrists, arms, knees, ankles and waists. They softened up the skins of wild animals and worked them prettily, making leathern aprons to wear. Most of the girls smeared their bodies over with a fine powdered soft stone mixed with oil or fat, while nearly all the boys plastered white paint over themselves, and the little children tattoed their bodies with pointed sticks, or made circular burns on their arms.

On the morning of the party — Christmas Day — the mothers anxiously gave a final touch to their children's toilet by a special coating of grease, and sent the boys off to catch rats, mice and birds with which to delight their guests' appetites, and instructed all — for the hundredth time — not to forget to be especially polite to the Chief.

As Petrus' and George's ponies galloped up to the Chief's kraal — or the "Great Place," as it was called — they could see long strings of gayly decked little black children all hurrying from the different huts over to the "Great Place," which was, of course, by far the largest of all the kraals in the great semi-circle which looked for all the world like a gigantic fairy-ring of mushrooms with elongated stalks — for their upright poles reached as much as five feet before their tops were lashed to the thatched roof, with "monkey-rope."

Arriving at the "Great Place," all the laughing, fat, little black children swarmed about the narrow doorway, which was but a foot and a half high, then got down on their hands and knees and crawled in the kraal.

Petrus and George struggled through after them. Inside, the air was dense with smoke which made their eyes smart. About the mud-walls rested bright bunches of assegais, and small stabbing knives were stuck into the thatch. In single file all the children walked up to the Chief, by whose side stood the sturdy little "Bull of the Kraal"—or "Crown Prince" as we might say—and pausing a moment before him, saluted him with the word: "Bayette!" which means "Great Chief." Then, discovering Petrus and George, they crowded around them, yelling: "Azali!" "Azali!" which is just Kafir for "A present! A present!" Knowing what to expect, Petrus came prepared with a large box of "Candy Lakkers" which he presented to the little "Bull of the Kraal."

Then came the most important event of the party—the refreshments, which consisted of such delicate titbits as fried mice, locusts, mutton, goat, and old hens, which had been roasted over the embers.

After all had been gobbled up, various violent games, such as "Horses," "Wolf," and so on, were played by the children. Many of the bigger boys crawled about frightening the younger ones, pretending to be lions.

Petrus and George, beginning to tire of all this, were about to thank their kind host, the Chief, for their pleasant afternoon, mount their ponies and strike out for home. They peered anxiously through the kraal door to see if their ponies were all right. It was nearly dark. George looked anxious as he recalled his promise to his Aunt Edith. "We must go!" he said to Petrus.

"All right, George. I think so, too. Come on. It's late!"

Just at that moment there appeared the "Great Wife," as she was called. Of all the Chief's many wives she was his favorite—the "wife of his heart"—and the mother of the little "Bull of the Kraal," who was heir to the chieftainship.

"Mabiliana" was her name. Petrus and George had long heard of her beauty. They had heard, too, that five men had been assegaied before she became the undisputed property of the gallant Chief, who had paid the large "lobola" of fifty of his fattest oxen for her.

All the pickaninnies hailed her appearance with a great shout of joy. They crowded about her, clamoring for "A story!" "A story!"

"Just one moment longer, Petrus—just till she begins her story," promised George, as Mabiliana gracefully seated herself before thechildren who quickly ranged themselves in a circle on the floor about her feet.

Her dress was in keeping with her beauty. A broad band of blue and white beads encircled her forehead, while hanging in a gracefully pendant curve over her eyelids, sparkled another string of the same white beads giving to her eyes a languid look. About her slender round throat were negligently hung many more sparkling strings. Bead and brass bracelets encircled her wrists, arms and slender ankles, where also was noticed a fringe of monkey's hair, while fastened about her waist was a little leathern apron, tastefully ornamented with blue, red and white beads.

"Which shall it be, children? The 'Story of the Shining Princess' or 'Nya-Nya Bulembu,' 'The Fairy Frog,' or 'The Beauty and the Beast'?" asked Mabiliana, very gracefully taking a pinch of snuff from time to time.

"The Beauty and the Beast!" shouted all the little blacks with one voice. That story is a great favorite with Kafir children.

"Then 'The Beauty and the Beast' it shall be," sweetly assented the young Kafiress.

Mabiliana was really distressed at being urged to tell a fairy-story by daylight. To do so—according to all Kafir traditions—was to invoke the wrath of a wicked spirit. Many a beauty had been known to become as hideous as an "Imbula," or ogre, after that. But rather than refuse the children, many of whom she loved dearly, Mabiliana decided to tell the story, then she asked for a piece of glass. Tucking this quickly into her hair, to ward off the evil, she combed her woolly locks over it, using the long mimosa thorn which she carried stuck through her ear. Then carefully replacing the thorn, and, taking a pinch of snuff, she began her story.

The children listened in breathless, big-eyed silence. Spellbound they held their breath as the story reached the terrible moment when the "Mollmeit" appeared—the monster "who killed and ate little girls, and—"

Outside the loud sound of approaching hoof-beats stopping at the kraal startled the boys.

"Oh, it's daddy come for me!" whispered conscience-stricken George to Petrus, as he burst from the kraal into the inky blackness outside, calling:

"Daddy! Where are you?"

Petrus dashed after him. He heard one terrified shriek, followed by the thud, thud, thud, of a galloping horse's hoofs—growing fainter and fainter, then silence, but for the loud cackling and barking of the hens and dogs.

"George! Where are you? George! George!" frantically called Petrus, peering through the inky darkness in every direction.

Only the commotion among the fowls and dogs broke the dead silence.

"George! George!" louder called Petrus, in despair.

There came no answer.

Petrus looked about for the ponies. There they were both quietly standing just where he had left them. Shobo—the Bushboy—rushed up.

"Cluck, cluck, click, click—nhlpr—nh!" he cried out, gesticulating wildly to Petrus, and pointing far off to the west.

"Oh, my master! My master!" cried Mutla, galloping breathlessly up. "The Zulu! The Zulu! He got Master George!"

Petrus' foot struck against something hard. He shuddered. There lay a six-foot long, iron-tipped assegai. One just like it fell into the flying cart that day. He had it yet. The horrible truth came home to him—George was gone!

"Quick, Ferus!" cried Petrus, springing into the saddle with the assegai under one arm. Ferus shot over the ground at a slashing pace. Soon his master was within sight of Lieutenant Wortley's home. The soft glow of evening lights came from the windows. From one there came the sparkle of many little candlelights. They were on a tree. Petrus could see George's Aunt Edith carefully arranging the presents for the evening party—George's party.

They reached the door. Petrus sprang from Ferus and dashed up the steps, crying—

"Oh, Lieutenant Wortley! George is gone!"

CHAPTER VIII

A STORM ON THE DRAKENSBERG

Only low-growling Hector and little Theunis, looking down from his bedroom window, saw them silently depart. In the cold gray dawn-light Petrus waved a quick "good-by" up to the wondering child and they were off.

Long before sun-up, faithful Mutla had had the three ponies up-saddled and waiting under the orchard trees. He had strapped a small roll containing a pair of blankets and a rain-coat to the front of his master's saddle, and to that of the lead-horse he had tied a large piece of biltong, or sun-dried meat, a good supply of biscuit and coffee, and fastened an iron kettle in which to make it. Petrus had hurriedly pressed a Testament into the pocket of his moleskin trousers, and made sure that the two Mausers they were carrying were well oiled. There was no time to lose. They hoped to overtake Dirk on the road.

True, the lieutenant had offered a reward of five hundred pounds in gold to the one who returned his little son alive to him; but love for his little English friend and neighbor was the real motive for Petrus' suddenly planned flight over the dangerous Drakensberg Mountains.

All night long the lieutenant, heading a large searching party of his friends and neighbors, with half a hundred Kafirs, had scoured the neighboring woods and hills for some trace of George. In a fever of excitement, Aunt Edith, who spent the night at "Weltefreden," declared it was her belief that the poor boy must have been killed—assegaied—or thrown into some stream and perhaps devoured alive by the crocodiles.

Aunt Johanna's fears, too, were grave, and Magdalena plainly informed Hercules that there could be no happy wedding on New Year's Day unless little George was captured from the Zulu, and brought home alive and well before that time.

So all night the searching party, headed by the lieutenant, Petrus and Hercules, carried great torches of flaming grass and tree-branches, and flooded with light every deep game-pit, every clump of trees, kopje, and river bank. But no answer had come. So, at sunrise, the party broke up and returned home. Grief stricken, the lieutenant with the aid of Hercules, immediately formed a large well-armed party of picked Kafirs and made straight for the Kalahari Desert. There it was he had first seen the threatening Zulu. There it was he would no doubt return with George—and perhaps take his revenge by selling George into slavery to the Bechuanas. It was a long trip back to that deadly "thirst-land." They had left by sunrise. Already the party was well on its way.

But Petrus remembered one most significant remark of his Aunt Kotie's. He remembered her telling him that Dirk had come to her from Natal, where he had been one of a gang of Zulu dock-hands, piling lumber at the wharf at Durban. She had also told him that Dirk's people belonged to the great military kraal at Ekowe, in Zululand, near the Tugela River. Petrus believed Dirk was making his escape with George, taking the shortest cut back over the robber-infested Drakensberg Mountains to the docks.

Moreover, Mutla—who, like all Kafirs, was an expert at "following the spoor"—had "spoored" the hoof-marks of the Zulu's horse from the very door of the Chief's kraal. The ground was still moist from recent rains, and Mutla's keen eyes and quickness of perception had detected the grass bent down, and pebbles scattered leaving the wet side up-turned, and often the whole hoof-press of the horse clearly stamped in the soft ground.

Mutla was certain he was following the very road the Zulu had taken. The hoof-marks led southwards, towards the Drakensberg Mountains. So for two days they traveled over the monotonous grasslands of the Orange Free State with its interminable thorn-bushes, until finally, as they neared the base of the mountains, the spoor was crossed and re-crossed by the cloven hoof indentations of the eland, the slipper-like footprints of the giraffe, and the immense circular depressions made by the elephant, with now and then, to their horror, the dreaded print of the lion's paw. Petrus and Mutla kept their rifles ready for instant use. As the trees grew thicker the whir of wings and sudden flash of brilliant plumage told them that feathered game was not wanting.

Suddenly there was a mighty rustling in the underbrush with the sound of breaking branches among the trees close to them. Mutla's pony buck-jumped, carrying his rider headlong to the ground. Five elephants burst through the trees and dashed down an embankment on the left of the road to the water, where, with mighty gurglings and splashings, the monsters threw the water from their trunks in streams over their bodies, and a little baby elephant ran about with a tree branch playfully held in his trunk.

"Oh, Baas, I thought it was lions sure!" exclaimed the frightened Kafir.

"The big fellows didn't even see us, Mutla, and I don't think they would have charged us if they had. But let us water our ponies and hasten on our way."

They came out of the forest into a narrow and very winding road, and advanced at a tripping pace. Soon they were zigzagging up the face of the Drakensberg—the loftiest and grandest mountain range in all South Africa. Soon the darkness of night would overtake them. Something made them think of robbers. But Petrus was not afraid. He was a daring rider. His horsemanship had received high praise from the lieutenant himself, and he had marked skill with weapons. He knew the position of the sun at all hours of the day, and of the stars by night. They could not stray far from their way. Mutla had Arab blood in his veins. With his keen, piercing eyes he could see all the dangerous roads and precipices in the dark.

Ferus suddenly trembled violently. Petrus gave a quick glance into the trees close by. Crouching at full length, far out on a branch overhanging the stream, was a leopard glaring down, ready to spring. Instantly Petrus' rifle was at his shoulder. The report soundedthrough the forest, and the "tiger-cat," as Mutla called it, fell with a splash into the water below.

"Oh, my master, lions sure about here," protested the still frightened Mutla, as Petrus dismounted and began to cut down branches with which to build a fire. With sun-down had come complete darkness there in the depths of the tropical mountain forest.

"Fires are our best protection against wild beasts. Come, let us prepare our supper, and sleep, for to-morrow's journey is to be a long one."

Petrus fastened the ponies to a tree by their head-stalls, while Mutla piled on branches and sticks, making the little fire crackle and blaze up warmly as they prepared and ate their supper.

Then, using their saddles for pillows, with their rifles at their sides and the blankets stretched on the ground under them, they fellasleep, but only for a short time. Soon they awoke to find the forest flooded with bright moonlight. It was light as day. Petrus reached for a high branch of a native tree. This he bent down and broke off a piece about four feet long.

"I'm making a 'knob-kerrie,' Mutla. It may be useful to-morrow in killing snakes." Some, like the venomous mamba, are nine feet long. Mutla watched Petrus as he skillfully formed the knob at one end. Then, aiming it at an imaginary beast far off among the trees, Petrus sent it spinning over and over through the air with a twirling motion, until it fell with a crash that reverberated throughout the forest. Instantly the whole forest was alive. Mutla grew nervous as he watched the dark forms everywhere mysteriously moving through the trees.

"Keep your gun ready, Mutla," advised Petrus.

"That I will, Baas," promptly answered the black boy.

After their night's rest, the ponies made good time early next morning, climbing the ascending jagged roads. The path dropped at times into deep mountain valleys, then rose to greater heights until at last they reached the famous "De Beer's Pass,"—which led across the lofty peaks of the "Dragon Mountains," to the Natal side. Only after hours of difficult scaling did the riders succeed in reaching this commanding ledge, from which they obtained their first view of "fair Natal," stretching far below in all its beauty.

More and more lonely and wild became the road as the descent was begun. Strange they had not overtaken Dirk yet. But they might at any moment. Gaunt crags rose all about them. From the trees overhead there came a flapping, hissing, struggling noise. Mutla gasped and uttered a shriek, as swooping savagely down upon him from its lofty nest was an immense eagle of the "man-eating" species. Its wings must have measured six feet from tip to tip. One blow from Petrus' knob-kerrie sent the "man-eater" flying from his prey.

"You have had a narrow escape, Mutla," said Petrus, springing into the saddle, as a great peal of thunder sounded and the sky darkened suddenly. Scarcely could they get into their rain-coats before the storm broke. First one, then the other of the ponies, slipped on the soft, wet ground, but quickly recovered themselves. The ponies continued to lose their footing as they made the irregular, uncertain descending slopes, often passing by dangerous ledges, dongas and pools. So dark had it grown they could not see their pony's ears in front of them.

"Follow me, my master, you're going wrong," came Mutla's caution now and then, as they traveled on through the blackness.

Late in the afternoon the storm ceased and the sun shone dimly. The dripping boys wondered where they were, and how far they had traveled, when a lone rider passed them and — to their delight — told them they were among the monarch trees at the base of the mountain. He pointed the way to the nearest human habitation, the hut of a kind Kafir missionary where they could have supper and pass the night.

Petrus was glad to learn that the kind Kafir was a very intelligent but aged missionary who spoke the Zulu language. He lighted a fire for them to dry themselves, while Petrus related to him the events of the day and why he had undertaken so dangerous a journey.

"In search of the little English boy? The Natal papers are full of descriptions of the Zulu, the offer of the reward, etc. Only yesterday just such a powerfully built Zulu, dragging a little lame white boy by the hand, came begging food at my door. When I began to questionhim he left suddenly, but not before I learned from him that he was on his way to Durban."

"Oh! That must have been Dirk! The boy must have been George!" cried Petrus, with sparkling eyes. "Mutla, up-saddle the ponies at once! We have no time to lose!"

"No, wait until morning. Your ponies are tired. The road from here to Durban is a rough one at best. Even the bravest would not be foolhardy enough to undertake it by night," insisted the old missionary.

"You are right. We will sleep to-night. In the early morning, long before you are up, we will be far on our way. Good-night, and thank you for all your kindness," said Petrus, handing the kind Kafir a sovereign to aid him in his work.

"Then 'good-night,' my boy, I wish you success and God-speed."

CHAPTER IX

A ZULU WAR-DANCE

It was a glorious December morning. Petrus and Mutla were again in their saddles. Ladysmith and a near-by ostrich farm were soon left far behind. Then they forded the historic Tugela, which barely came up to their ponies' knees.

They made good play at a swinging gallop, threading their way in and out through Natal's tree-covered hills.

The country through which they were hastening was of indescribable beauty—a veritable fairyland with its rushing streams, beautiful forests of sweet-scented evergreens, graceful palm-trees and masses of strange and beautiful wildflowers.

Petrus and Mutla were in the land of the black man, from the melancholy-faced Hindoo cooly to the blackest of black Zulus.

Gliding nimbly in and out through the bushes, or creeping slyly up in the tall grass, were bunches of swift-footed Zulus. Petrus shuddered, and closely scanned each black face for Dirk's. Thousands of their beehive-like kraals were thickly scattered over every hillside they were passing.

"Look out for Dirk, Mutla. We may pass him on the road at any moment," sternly cautioned Petrus, as they hastened on through Natal's tropical valleys and uplands.

They paused at Pietermaritzburg. There the papers were full of the story and the offer of the large reward, but no trace of the stolen boy. Realizing that Durban must be reached at once, if Dirk was to be overtaken, they changed their pace into an easy gallop and dashed on their way towards the coast, past many large banana and sugar-cane plantations. A cooling breeze was brushing the hillsides, for it had rained hard during the night.

It was only about noon when they reached Natal's beautiful seaport—the "Pearl of South African Cities," as Durban has been called. Petrus made straight for the land-locked harbor. Above—on one of these beautiful terraced hillsides overlooking the Indian Ocean—he could see the handsome residences of the Berea, where dwelt Durban's prosperous business men.

"Dirk would neither be working there, nor as a jinrickshaw-boy in the busy streets of the town," thought Petrus, as they hurried on to the docks. There he found hundreds of powerfully built, broad-chested, coal-black Zulus, all hard at work piling great beams of wood in orderly rows on the wharf. They sang as they worked. Petrus scrutinized every ebony face but saw no little white b among them.

"Look close, Mutla. Dirk worked here on this dock once. He may be here now."

Just at that moment a gust of wind sent a Durban morning paper fluttering against Ferus' feet. Dropping quickly to the ground, Petrus caught it before it was gone.

"Mutla!" he exclaimed excitedly. "Quick, Mutla! We're going to Zululand! We can reach there before dark if we try. The paper says that Dirk was seen working here on this dock late yesterday afternoon, and that he suddenly disappeared with the boy in the direction of the swamps of Saint Lucia Bay, where many are following him. But Dirk will never go that far. He will turn aside and make straight for his kraal at Ekowe. Come! We'll get George yet!"

Petrus hastily sent the following telegram to Lieutenant Wortley:

"Am safe. Shall reach Dirk's kraal at Ekowe, in Zululand, before night. Hope to start home with George by morning.

PETRUS."

The heart of Zululand was but a few hours away. With a word to Ferus, and a spur-thrust to Mutla's brown pony, they dashed forward at a swinging pace. Ahead of them, as they topped each rise, rose the romantic hills of Zululand—the clear atmosphere making them plainly visible. Through the trees on their right every now and then they got blue glimpses of the Indian Ocean.

Once Ferus swerved and trembled violently. There—lying coiled up in a ring in the center of the road—Petrus saw a great hooded Cobra, the largest and most deadly of South African reptiles. Ferus was leaping in terror. Before Petrus could rein him in, the viper rose on its tail, hissed, and made two strikes at Ferus' feet, then escaped through the grass into a hole at the root of an old tree.

On they sped through the beautiful coast forests. Every now and then bunches of dark-eyed, woolly-pated, naked Zulus, with skincarosses thrown over one shoulder, appeared and as suddenly disappeared. No sooty face missed Petrus' quick eye. Once he heard the shouting and laughter of a group of good-natured young Zulus ahead of him. With glistening bodies they were emerging from the clear waters of a spruit into which they had just plunged themselves. Presently, from out the bush on his left, there stole a huge coal-black lone Zulu carrying an iron-tipped assegai. Instantly Petrus' rifle was at his shoulder. But it was not Dirk.

In the gathering dusk the roadway was becoming full of dangerous turns and slopes. Ferus never made a false step. Over many a bridge the ponies clattered on their way. At last they were in Zululand, once the land of "Chief Chaka," and of powerful "Ketchwayo," whose warriors proudly called him "Strong Mighty Elephant." It was in Zululand that Empress Eugénie's son, the Prince Imperial, had been slain by the fierce blacks.

The glare of the setting sun was behind them as they turned in the direction of the famous Zulu military kraals of Ekowe. Cutting through the undergrowth of rank luxuriance, they went at top speed. Often the Zulu grass met above their ponies' ears. Presently they emerged into a more open, grassy space where they passed a half-wild herd of Zulu cattle contentedly feeding. They were beautiful little creatures.

"Mutla, we must be very near the Ekowe kraals!" excitedly exclaimed Petrus, "otherwise this herd of Zulu cattle would hardly be grazing here! Look out for Dirk!"

They had gone but a short distance farther when three mounted Zulus with strings of birds around their necks, rode slowly up, glared at them and passed on their way. In a little while their ears caught the sound of girls' chattering voices. Then a group of dusky Zulu beauties, scantily clad in skins and beads, strolled across their path and disappeared. Soon they passed whole troops of cunning little black urchins laughing and playing together. Petrus slackened his pace somewhat. One little group stopped to stare in wide-eyed wonder at the white riders. Then one little naked savage came running directly up to the ponies in the most friendly fashion.

A quick low whistle brought Ferus to a full stop. She patted the pony affectionately, and, smiling up to Petrus, chattered something to him in Zulu, which was equivalent to: "How do you do, great white Chief?"

Petrus handed the youngster a sixpence and asked: "Dirk? Where's Dirk?"

"Dirk? Want Dirk?" repeated the friendly child, with a brightening look and quick nod of recognition of the name. "Dirk there—kraals!" she gladly explained, pointing down the road, then ran laughingly back to her companions with the sixpence.

"Oh, Mutla! Dirk surely must be here! Keep in the shadow of the trees. Everything depends upon our not being seen."

"Yes, Baas," answered Mutla somewhat nervously, as they began to wend their way through the city of two hundred or more armed kraals arranged in several great circles—one lying within the other like so many great garlands spread over the grass. Shields and spears were everywhere stuck into the thatch of the numerous large beehive-like huts made of wattles or poles, the upper ends of which were bent over and lashed together with a strong vine called "monkey-rope." The lower ends were firmly fastened into the ground. They had indeed reached the far-famed Zulu military kraals of Ekowe, where dwelt the garrison of the King's army. But for a pack of yelping, barking dogs, which dashed viciously out at the pony's heels, all seemed silent and deserted.

"Turn back among the trees!" commanded Petrus. "We must get out of here quickly!" The ground under the trees into which they had abruptly turned for shelter was literally covered with strange trophies of Zulu prowess with wild beasts—leopards' skulls, Rhino horns, lions' teeth and claws, jackals' tails and skins, ostriches' eggs and feathers, with great heaps of bones and broken assegais. An array of game was hanging from the trees.

Suddenly the sound of hundreds of voices reached them from far in the distance.

"Listen, Mutla! The sound comes from the direction of that great open plateau, far across there. What can it all be about?" exclaimed Petrus, whose heart was filled with new hope. Cautiously emerging to the edge of the woods, they beheld a scene to make one's blood run cold. There — far across on the opposite plateau — charging in a frenzy of excitement, brandishing their battle-axes and assegais, yelling and whirling their knob-kerries, was the whole garrison of mounted Zulus. As Petrus and Mutla watched, their yells broke forth into their ancient "war-song" to which Ketchwayo's victorious armies had marched.

"Mutla, they surely can't be on the warpath! It must be an imaginary battle they are fighting. We must slip up closer and closer, keeping well out of sight ourselves, but where we can see if Dirk is among them. It will soon be too dark to see. Look well, Mutla!"

"Master afraid?" questioned the paling Kafir.

"Afraid, Mutla? Why should we be afraid? Are we not both well armed?" answered the Boer boy, as they crept closer and closer, taking advantage of every tree and wooded knoll to conceal their approach. Soon they were within forty yards, and evidently unobserved. The warriors' ox-hide shields and high-poised assegais gleamed in the setting sun, as, stamping the earth furiously, the whole yelling mass made another wild charge. Petrus kept his hand on his rifle and a bullet in his mouth. The Zulu's eyes blazed.

"Oh, Mutla, look! Look quick! The big Zulu there is Dirk! And, Mutla, that little bit of a lame boy in the midst of the 'war dance' is — ! It's! Look! Dirk banged him over the head with his shield. He's crying. Oh, if only we could let him know in some way that we are here. He's looking this way! I am going to wave my hat! Quick, Mutla, wave to him! There, he saw us! He waved his arm to me! He's smiling now. See him?" Petrus wanted to shout for joy.

"Yes, Master. But how dare we get him away from Dirk?"

"To-night, when Dirk is fast asleep, George will come to this very tree where he saw us. We can't remain here. It's too exposed. But he will find this note. I'll stick it right through a high tree-branch here — where he'll be sure to see it. I'll make it so big that he can't miss it. There now. Quick! Let us make our escape back among the trees, Mutla!"

Scarcely had Mutla followed Petrus back out of sight than the entire shrieking, savage regiment swept down over the very spot where, but a moment before, their ponies had been standing.

"Dirk didn't see us, Mutla. He didn't look this way at all. But I saw George look right at the big note up on the tree. He'll come."

Long was the night. At last Petrus thought he heard the joyful sound of two or three swiftly running steps behind him. Petrus listened again, but he was not certain, when — "Petrus! Petrus!" he heard close behind him.

Springing from Ferus, Petrus turned to search for the voice.

"George! George!" he cried softly in joy, as a little lame boy came limping out from behind a big tree and bounded forward into his arms.

"Petrus! Take me home! Take me home!" he cried. "Quick, before Dirk comes! Dirk tried to make a Zulu of me, Petrus, and — "

A great rushing sound of wheels drowned the rest of George's sentence. It was a large motor-car — for even in far-off Africa they have automobiles — with two armed passengers, which swung directly up to them and halted.

"Oh, DADDY! FATHER! FATHER!" cried George, throwing himself into his father's arms.

"GEORGE! GEORGE! my precious boy!" cried the lieutenant, seizing his child with a look of great joy. "Here, Petrus, jump into the car beside Hercules. You have won George's and my everlasting gratitude. Mutla, take this money and bring the ponies home by freight. Good-by. We're off for home!"

"Good-by, Mutla, and thank you for coming with me," called back Petrus, as the big car whirled out of sight.

CHAPTER X

PETRUS THE HERO

It was on the afternoon of New Year's Day—the day of Magdalena's wedding—that they reached home. It was one of those bright midsummer afternoons for which the Transvaal is famous. From the windows and doors of "Weltefreden" soft lights glowed, and the merry strains of fiddles and an accordion reached the ears of Lieutenant Wortley, Petrus, and a happy little English boy sitting between them, as the big car whirred up to the old farmhouse stoop.

The long row of saddles against the red brick wall told of the large number of gayly decked riders who had already arrived—many of whom were standing in groups outside, shaking hands, drinking coffee and discussing Petrus' heroism, as they watched the unloading of Cape carts, wagonettes, spiders, horse and ox-wagons full of Dutch vrouws and children, whose bright dresses flashed gayly in the sunlight.

Every now and then the crack of a whip announced the arrival of Boer families of greater means, in conveyances ostentatiously drawn by four, six, or even eight horses, according to their wealth. The men-folks, in tight patent-leather oxfords, courteously helped their showily dressed vrouws and daughters to alight, while Hottentot nurses took care of the blond little girls in bright prints, and their little brothers in new mole-skins. Hercules had already arrived. He had hastened on by train, when the lieutenant had paused at Ladysmith to consult a doctor about George's lame foot.

"Oh, there's Aunt Kotie's motor!" exclaimed Petrus, as he and George bounded into the big house—Petrus straight into Aunt Johanna'soutstretched arms, while George rushed to his Aunt Edith, who nearly smothered him with hugs and kisses.

"Petrus is home! PETRUS IS HOME!" flew from one to another until the whole gathering had heard the good news. All knew he had won the "reward," for Aunt Kotie had brought the latest Johannesburg paper giving the full account. All had been thrilled by the story of his daring rescue of George. Now that he was safely home again, every one present crowded about to shake hands with their young hero. Scarcely had the blushing boy recovered from this ovation when he found himself enveloped in the arms of the happy bride who, with Hercules, had just returned from the church.

Then Lieutenant Wortley spoke:

"As you all know, our brave Petrus has won the reward offered for George's rescue. The amount has been on deposit in gold in the National Bank of South Africa as advertised. Let me therefore take this opportunity of making good my promise—here before this gathering of his friends and relatives—by now writing out for Petrus an order on the National Bank of South Africa for the five hundred pounds he has so well won.

"Much as I rejoice at the finding of my own little boy, Petrus is the real hero, and I want to express the overwhelming sense of gratitude which both George and I feel towards this brave young lad.

"Petrus, there is no one we would rather have had win this reward than you—especially as it is to be the means of your some day coming to England to take your college course at Oxford with George.

"We return to England at once. My country needs my services at the front. But in the years to come there will never be a more welcome visitor at our old home in London than our daring little Boer friend from 'Weltefreden.'"

"Good-by, Lieutenant Wortley! Good-by, George dear!" stammered Petrus—his eyes sparkling and his sun-burnt cheeks aglow with pride, as, waving a last farewell to the English friends he had grown to love, he dashed from the room amid a great clapping of hands and more congratulations.

He was glad to make his escape up to his own little room—to think. He had so much to think about. Oh, everything was possible now! Mutla's poor sick brother should be saved from death in the Kimberley diamond mines at once. And, as for his own great trip over the new "Cape to Cairo" road? Why, yes! He could now take Aunt Johanna and the whole family with him. Then there was London! His college course at Oxford, England, and, best of all, he would again see George! Wonderful dreams for the future thronged the mind of our little Boer cousin as he gazed from his window towards the star-lit heavens in the midst of which burned the Southern Cross.

THE END